FOR T
WHICH
CAN NOT
B
RESTORED

# 복원되지 못한 것들을 위하여

**PARK WANSEO**
Translated by Soobin Kim

'Pays well,' said Hahm, signing the receipt.

'Rubbish,' I said tartly, looking up from gnawing at the cap of my ballpoint pen.

Hahm was a poet as young as my daughter. I'd been polite all day since we'd only just met. I still don't know the reason for my sudden change in tone. Some anxiety disorder, perhaps. That's how my kids jokingly explained the occasional nail-biting or pen-chewing, anyway.

But, as Hahm said, the remuneration did in fact tend towards the generous side. A women's magazine half-packed with adverts would offer a third of this sum for sifting unscreened entries. And these entries, in turn, had already been crisply screened and whittled down to a readable handful. We only had to read a few each, so I might say excessive, even—not just generous. And further, the magazine was largely unmarketable. It was published by a public investment agency to hammer in the government agenda and would be rebuffed by intellectuals, who tended to give government mouthpieces a wide berth. Municipal offices may have displayed some copies, copies that they either got for free or were pressed to purchase, but the magazine had a slim chance of survival on its own revenues alone. In the wake of the June 29 Declaration, and with a presidential election ahead,

8   a groundswell of aspirations ran across a newly enfranchised
citizenry. So, I wasn't much bothered by working with the
publication but thought a government-issued periodical still
warranted a degree of scepticism.

'Extravagant office for a magazine director, too' said Hahm,
who strode across the marble floors, mugwort-green and as
smooth as glass, with the fetching gait of a runway model, then
turned to wait for me. I crept along behind her, still unnerved from
having tweaked my ankle last year.

'A brassy sort, obviously.'

The offices were sumptuous, authoritarian even. Hardly what
you'd expect from such a magazine. We were to read our assigned
pile of entries on the spot, each select two, then award the winner,
runner-up, and special commendation. This still took some time.
Throughout the two hours we were there, we didn't see the editor-
in-chief once. Nobody seemed to know where the boardroom was
except for one staff editor.

'Tea?' Hahm asked.

There was a teahouse across from the elevator where we
stepped out.

'We just had some.'

'Right. If you didn't bring your car, I can drive you. I'm headed
in the same direction?'

'I don't own a car. Don't worry about it. I have some errands
to run while I'm here'

This needless lie cost me a ride, and I padded towards the
subway entrance. I had been on edge all day  with Hahm and felt
calmer by myself. Still, I bit my nails on the subway, and at the
supermarket, when the sight of the payment envelope in my bag
sent me into a paroxysm of embarrassment and rage, I—to hell
with it—started snapping up unnecessary stuff.

'Mum seems stressed, again,' my daughter said, unfurling the grocery bags. I would excuse these impulsive sprees as a way of letting off steam. I simply shrugged at her like a westerner, which did nothing to temper the bottled-up shame and simmering anger within me.

Three days later, I was leafing through the morning paper when the phone rang.

'Mum, it's for you. From *The Nation Ahead*.'

'Should've said I'm not in...' I muttered and took the receiver. It was the editorial assistant from the magazine.

'The winner indeed asked to drop out, much as you said he would. We have a fallback, though, thanks to you, but I just wanted to keep you in the loop.'

The assistant, normally unflappable and all-business, sounded slightly excited at my foresight. I took the tone for mockery and started to sputter out of humiliation.

'And you just took no for an answer?'

'Of course not. Our editor went down there and stayed the night to persuade him, but he wouldn't budge.'

'Well, isn't that peculiar. Writing it must have been an excruciating effort and now he doesn't want it published at all? If it's reprisals he's afraid of, you should've said we'd go to the wall for him, that things have changed.'

'Our editor, too, was keen to run it and tried all kinds of things to persuade him. But the writer insisted. It's a no-go, the story was as invented, a fiction, and as such would violate the rules of the competition. What could we say?'

'I could vouch for the story's authenticity... Are you sure this isn't just an excuse to spike the story? It's plenty possible with *The Nation Ahead*.'

'How dare... We would never—You know how hard we've tried

to keep up with the times!'

She had expressed something similar delivering the manuscripts—anticipation for finding a piece that challenged the conventions of a government-issued periodical, rather than the usual hackwork—with the look of someone clutching at straws. It seemed a futile gesture to try to reverse a long cemented reputation with one essay, but her hope drew my pity. I, for one, didn't regard essays as much more than an air vent for grievances. But, perhaps because the cash prizes were substantial, all shortlisted entries had turned out to be excellent and had dealt with rich subject matter.

When the quality of entries is uniformly high, selecting the winner can be difficult. But this time, 'Restoration', as it was titled, was peerless. Usually it can be a slog, sifting through a mediocre stack, but electrifying work such as this can set off white-hot excitement in me. Outwardly I had remained calm and handed 'Restoration' and another entry to Hahm for her decision. Hahm gave me her picks and said, 'They're all up to par. But no standouts.'

Which meant a surefire win for 'Restoration'. I was grinning contentedly inside with anticipation but screwed on a straight face while I scanned Hahm's own selections.

Halfway through 'Restoration' Hahm uttered, 'You have quite an eye.'

'No, we both do.'

So we had easily agreed on the winner. Hahm chose the runner-up and special commendation. I was indifferent to the rest, having found a work to my liking.

Ginseng tea and fruit were then served. For having judged a minor magazine's competition, one hardly known for providing a breakthrough for writers in either literary fiction or nonfiction, we were overly satisfied. In fact, my satisfaction touched on elation.

'No one would've come forward with something like that in the past...' Hahm said. 'Especially not some country bumpkin like this guy.'

And that was it. We were pleased not just with the entry itself, but with a new era in which such a story could be told. The past to which Hahm referred was mere months ago, before the June 29 Declaration.

'Restoration' is about two fraudulent legislative elections, pre- and post-Yushin. It's written by a village chieftain, so high up in the family pedigree that even to hoary village elders he is kingmaker, envisioning a sea change that would save the village from ruin. It so happens that the only university-enrolled student of the village is studying animal husbandry, and from discussions with the youth he concludes that prosperity hinged on a shift from agriculture to livestock. The transition could not be self-propelled in such an orthodox place, however. A reliable external force would have to be harnessed to fix a collective vision onto a brighter future. And to hone in on knotty affairs like zoning, waterways, and public finance, that force would necessarily need to be drawn from a position of power.

So once election season starts, the chieftain, without thinking twice, aligns himself with a candidate of the ruling Republican Party. Because of the chief's serious clout throughout the electoral jurisdiction, no candidate would resist his overtures. The two sides bind magnetically together. The chieftain lays out his demands and in return receives a pledge from the candidate, who goes so far as to make campaign promises quoted verbatim from their dealings. The chieftain then throws himself fully into the campaign to leverage his influence to the candidate's benefit. He's initially disappointed by the candidate's sleaze but perseveres nonetheless with a single-minded determination to help his village.

As the election draws near and an extramarital scandal throws his candidate on the back foot, the chieftain hires the implicated woman to flitter through the district maniacally declaring herself to have been jilted by the rival candidate. These sordid scraps continue onto voting day. He employs every means of political manoeuvring at his disposal—ballot stuffing, proxy voting, vote rigging—every tactic that he's seen in the headlines. He then realises that, as a Republican organiser, there are no limits to what he could do. Nothing would be beyond the pale if it would ensure victory for his candidate.

The candidate, once elected, makes off without a word and the chieftain eventually follows him to Seoul. Now a lawmaker, he dismisses any action on the agreed-upon favours citing the uncertain political terrain and the dire state of the nation and such like. By the time the chieftain realises he has been hoodwinked, martial law is proclaimed and the national assembly is dissolved. The age of Yushin dawns.

The chieftain gloats over the lawmaker's short-lived tenure but hasn't entirely lost faith in him as indeed the nation does in fact spiral into a dire state shortly thereafter. During Yushin, he finagles the same promises out of the same Republican nominee and ruthlessly reemploys the same stunning tactics, like a rehearsed robbery sequence, for the nominee's eventual re-election. When his re-election becomes certain, the lawmaker again follows the playbook, once more spurning the demands of the chieftain who delivers him the victory.

This snapshot of events would sound entirely credible placed among the many corruption cases televised or printed in the newspapers every election cycle. To a judge with a firm belief that magazines are stuffed with well-worn narratives from rags-to-riches stories to woe-is-me misery memoirs, the piece stood out a mile. But what was even more outstanding was its particular rhetoric. In a manner both plainspoken and meticulous, it unspooled a full-face exposition of an electoral fraud that took place in a faraway district—so lucid that it elevated a peripheral incident to a distillation of a whole benighted era.

Its virtues were not in the prose itself, however. Rather, the absence of any innate talent for composition or carefully crafted sentences in fact worked in its favour. It was a matter-of-fact portrayal of not just how power orchestrates fraud, but how the ordinary people around power had cast themselves into a role in the general orchestration of fraud. There was no embellishment, no self-pity. In that way, it was different from the usual confessional, one that pretends to shoulder some blame while framing oneself as a hapless victim or scapegoat, the hypocrisy of which would enlighten nobody.

So its title 'Restoration' was wholly felicitous. Like how a shattered porcelain bowl is no more or less than the sum of its fragments, the author had pieced together the minutiae of what had happened with impressive recollection, which, given the elapsed decades, seemed impossible without having taken extensive notes. 'Restoration' charted the shared interests of the powerful and powerless, led the reader through a partnership to conspire in a power grab, and in doing so built a picture of the gravitational pull of corruption, but it was the painstaking documentation, that showed its author was still in command of himself, fully aware of precisely what he was doing at all times, which was the true feat of the piece.

'It's almost too good for this boring magazine,' Hahm said as we notified the editorial assistant of the winning entry.

'Watch it,' she shot back. 'Have you seen our circulation?'

'A bit dishonest to figure a million handouts as your circulation, isn't it?'

The two were friends from high school, they had said.

14    The assistant turned to me. 'If it has your seal of approval—and we know how exacting are your standards—then it should be a brilliant addition to our magazine.'

After that, I should have just politely taken the payment, risen to my feet, but my big mouth got the better of me. 'It might be good to have a back-up plan, just in case,' I said, drawing out my words.

'Just in case?'

'Oh, you know, in case the winner decides to withdraw or something. It's one thing to write an essay like this but it takes real guts to actually publish it,' I said, managing some semblance of seriousness after having blurted the first thought that entered my mind.

But the assistant and Hahm didn't seem to understand. They were just listening out of perfunctory respect for a washed-up, middle-aged author. Hahm didn't weigh in at all when I was picking out a back-up entry from the shortlist. As I sifted through the entries, regret and shame set deep in my stomach and festered into a kind of dysphoria. I couldn't have predicted how my big mouth would be so spot on.

By the time *The Nation Ahead* hit the bookshops, a newly elected president was at the helm and a new era seemed to be dawning. Freshly printed exposés arrived that ran the gamut from events as recent as the mass detentions at Samchung Re-education Camp to as far back as the 4.3 Massacres on Jeju Island, the Yeosu-Suncheon Rebellion, and the Geochang Massacres, right up to the Gwangju Uprising. An array of incidents forced into collective amnesia was now welling up and out into an outpouring of novels and nonfiction.

But 'Restoration' had been wiped clean from *The Nation Ahead*. Though nobody would have pointed the finger at me,

I would often retreat into inner monologues, telling myself it wasn't my fault, that my true intentions were blameless, despite my big mouth.

April 1988 passed by in a dizzying frenzy, stoked by parliamentary elections. The upcoming Olympics would bring the nation to fever pitch and I desperately wanted to scream down its restlessness.

On the day of Hansik, I used traffic as an excuse to put off a visit to the ancestral graves and eventually left on a weekday. It was not until then that I thought to stop by the address of the author on the way. I was confident I could find him without much effort. The memorial park I was to which I was heading was in Gwangalli, the same district as his fisheries. The country club and lake I passed on the way to the graves were described in his essay a few times.

Indeed, I arrived at Gwangalli's former chieftain, Yoon Jang-seon's place without too much difficulty. It was a skinny place with a corrugated asbestos-cement roof.

'Can I help you?' he said, sliding open the glass door.

He was just as dignified and well-trimmed as I'd pictured him. When finally he stood before me, my mind quickly depressurised and I blanked on anything to say. I wanted to get to the bottom of why 'Restoration' could not see the light of day. My guess was that he had been browbeaten into pulling the piece by the magazine's editors, which was the most satisfying explanation to me.

'Are you the writer that submitted to *The Nation Ahead* a few months ago?' I said carefully.

'Yes, but there's nothing more to say about that. We already agreed to say it never happened.' He said in a huff and tried to slide the door shut.

I pushed myself in, daringly, and sat on the threshold.

'Please, I'm not from the magazine. I'm the novelist responsible for judging the submissions.'

Only after I said this did he become less wary and his wife darted out of the kitchen and plunked down a rubber basin full of leafy greens. 'I told you that petition—or was it a complaint—would come back to bite you,' she barked. 'You have a wife who makes you three hot meals a day and two sons who send you money to spend every month. What more do you need? You have some nerve, to be slinging mud like that, after having told your children writing is no way to make a living.'

She had been listening. After this dressing down, Yoon cast his wife a sideways glance like a clingy child. I explained that, as the person who judged his essay, I wanted to know why such a well-written piece of work was withdrawn, out of curiosity and sympathy, and so had decided to drop by while I just happened to be casually in the neighbourhood.

But Yoon's wife, her inky lips pursed like a duck's bill, strung out her disbelief. 'Casually in the neighbourhood, eh? In this sleepy countryside? You must think we're in central Seoul!'

With patience, I tried to persuade them that I was just on my way back from the cemetery at the foot of the mountain ridges facing their house. Yoon was not sympathetic to my explanation, nor did he rebuke his wife, who stepped in and spoke for him. From his writing, I had expected a farmer with a sharp-edged sense of self. I was left sorely disappointed.

'I stopped him. I said, not in a million years. What of it?'

They seemed to begin to understand that I wasn't just snooping around, but they remained guarded.

With an indrawn breath, Yoon's wife uttered something unexpected. 'He's just like his father—looking for a cliff to drive off every time the world changes.'

Henpecked into silence, Yoon had a pitiful look on his face.

And Yoon's wife, who no longer regarded me with suspicion, related the uninspiring tale of the Yoon family's misshapen legacy.

Yoon's father was the village head when the Korean War broke. He stayed in hiding at its climax but stepped out of his bolthole at the news of the national troops' arrival. This was all well and good, until he was so moved by the sight of the South Korean flag flapping over a school that he started to cavort, cheering, 'Long live the Republic of Korea.' He was instantly shot dead. Guerrillas from the North Korean army were slinking in the sugarcane fields. South Korean soldiers stationed at the school returned fire, killed the guerrillas, and searched the fields in order to execute the rest. Had Yoon's father had any patience, said the wife, he could have spared not just his own life but the lives of those guerrillas too. He could have fled to the woods at night and even if he were to get caught and held as a political prisoner his life would have been spared.

All this she said pointedly—understandably so, given the absurd circumstances of her father-in-law's death. The incident hadn't caused much residual emotional anguish, but she had been bowled over by the subsequent turn of events that rendered the incident prescient in retrospect.

When Yoon started dredging up timeworn memories and writing them down page after page, she shrugged it off. She knew it was about the Republican Party, but they were long out of power for censorship to still be of concern. She was enticed by the prize money at first but quickly checked herself—folks like them would never have that kind of luck anyway. Still, she kept a spark of hope alive, in case they hear from Seoul someday about her husband's writing chops.

Then began the presidential elections. Once the village was plastered with campaign posters, Yoon's wife started twitching with apprehension. The candidate, a former politician who had almost invented the Republican Party, was in town to give a stump speech and one of the aides escorting him was the protagonist of her husband's essay. Nothing had changed. Since that very moment she had fretted about her husband's submission to the magazine.

Her husband was unable to dispel the curse of his heredity, she said. He would end up following his father down a foolish path, and like his dear father, his impatience and bad timing would spell doom. The couple quickly left the rally that day without even taking a complimentary meal ticket, driven out by guilt. And given that this was about the point in time when Yoon's essay was selected as the winner of our competition, it was now obvious it had been his wife who had tried to snuff out the source of their worries.

'He was against pulling the piece until the last minute,' she said. 'What a relief we didn't just take the cash. The guy he blew the whistle on is now in Seoul. He's one of the hangers-on of the candidate. They are both from the Republican Party, and everybody is saying he'll win, so no reason to assume otherwise. My husband will thank me later.'

This left no doubt as to whether they withdrew voluntarily. As the wife babbled on, Yoon kept his mouth shut and stayed put. These same scenes must have played out when the magazine's editor had made the trek down here. The course of events was now clear to me but I now struggled to believe the essay was the result of such a dopey man's own cerebration.

The site of the campaign was not far from where we were. I could hear the desperate shouts of politicians pandering to voters.

'We can get a free lunch over there,' Yoon's wife said to Yoon, as if signalling me to leave. An echo from the mike garbled the speech, but customary homilies about transparency were still just about intelligible.

Yoon stepped out of a room donning a bomber jacket and a fishing hat. 'Transparency, transparency. All this yapping about transparency,' he muttered. 'What's the use of transparency without restoration?'

He looked me in the eye by accident and smiled sheepishly, showing nicotine-stained front teeth. Only then was I finally convinced that he had written the piece and had titled it very deliberately.

**o**

As the parliamentary election results rolled in, I smiled bitterly as what Yoon's wife had said echoed in my mind. For the first time in a while, I stepped into a bookshop. Thankfully, many professional word-peddlers weren't as naive or cowardly as Yoon and his wife. Books I could not have imagined before the June 29 Declaration had poured into the market, jostling for spots on best-seller lists.

It wasn't just previously banned books. Novels that had come straight from the North caught my eye too. Roman à clefs and memoirs that dug for buried truths. Satires lampooning the Fifth Republic and the Yushin order, so riotously amusing that I was on the floor laughing upon reading just a few pages.

But inside, I wasn't truly rejoicing. Inside was a vast void, an unsettling itch for something.

I picked up a three-volume anthology of writers who had defected or been abducted to the north. It was edited by Q, a critic who had vigorously etched them into the annals of contemporary literature during a time when it was illegal to even mention their now fabled names. I studied the list of authors, as if under a spell. And my eyes finally alighted on one in particular: Song Sa-muk.

Song had lived on this side of the peninsula until the War. He was never considered a seminal author—like Jeong Ji-yong or Kim Kirim, for example—nor had he published any real hits, but Q's anthology gave his work gravitas in the period around the 1945 Liberation. His name, of course, was partially redacted. But I was grateful that a top-rate critic like Q had included him, like a swivel in our literary history.

In the decade before and after liberation, Song wrote novels that didn't inspire much awe but still offered some dry amusement. He used to teach at my high school, and in my bookish youth, when I first aspired to write fiction, being taught by a real novelist sent my heart aflutter. I longed for his approval and latched on to every word he said. The small compliments he doled out sowed the ambition to write the novels I would produce later on. I was delighted to see this great influence of mine finally figure in the literary landscape and overwhelmed to find his name fully restored.

Life felt sweeter and I sang effusive praise to the world as I skimmed the names that had been restored alongside Song's. But my satisfaction was short-lived. All that had been restored were the three syllables of his name. The title of the anthology was *Collected works of Defectors and Abductees*, neither of which he was. Song had been executed. Though I admit defection or abduction had a better ring to it than execution—left behind hope that they might still be alive—it was far from the truth in Song's case. How could I consider anything fully restored, when there hadn't been the slightest effort to find the original pieces? The truth couldn't be patched with substitutes, not even gold.

Several years ago, I was viewing a ceramics collection and found an inkwell that had been damaged when acquired. Its hues were of lustrous porcelain and its chipped edges had been gilded

over into a smooth curve. Despite its supple beauty, the collector
seemed disgruntled. The gold drew too much attention to itself
and could not replicate the original shape. So why cover it with
gold instead of something similar in material and colour? I asked.
It could've been imperceptible.

With a withering stare, the collector said, Then it wouldn't be
obvious that the inkwell had previously been damaged. It would
be deceptive.

It was then that I started to understand that he had filled
the cracks with gold not as a display of his own wealth but as an
indication of loss.

I was not much acquainted with Q but planned to visit him to
request Song's career end not in a disappearance but as complete
as it could be. Q might have had no reason to regard Song's work
as more than something that could stuff an anthology. A more
distinguished writer whose oeuvre could stand on its own might
call for special individual treatment, but how could I expect a busy
critic like Q to care about the fate of one unremarkable novelist?

Maybe he already knew the truth but hadn't given it much
thought. But I wanted to tell him regardless. It would change
nothing, but it was the truth. It was more gruesome than
abduction, but it was the truth and if he had been mistaken,
I would correct him. It was not my business if Q himself had
decided to paper over the facts or make an edit to a line in the
history he had written. That would be his own decision, to tell
him the truth was my duty. Perhaps far into the future he would
find more time to dig into exactly why an upstanding and ordinary
writer such as Song had been executed. If his own inquiry lay
before his eyes how intricately intertwined was the violent
madness of an era with the abject self-protection of intellectuals,
it would be a discovery of his own, not something I could be

blamed for. It was, after all, only a conjecture of mine.

Still, it was not easy to summon the will to confront Q. Correcting abduction to execution seemed a more than reasonable request. And it seemed worth thinking about how the surviving family, who had had to leave the truth interred all these years, would feel. Song was known to have been blessed with many children.

I was still dithering about the issue when I got a call out of the blue from Song's youngest son asking to meet. He said he had heard from his mother that a former student of his father's was a writer. His resemblance to Song was so striking I felt I reached a new understanding of what it means to live on through one's children.

'You seem—surprised.'

'You're the spitting image of your father.'

'Mum always says I take after him the most.'

'She must adore you.'

'Too old for that, I'm afraid.'

'Excuse me for asking, but how old are you?'

'Forty-three,' he said, before handing me a business card. He was a manager at a pharmaceutical company.

'Your father was about your age when he was my teacher.'

'Yes, I suppose so. He was forty-four when he was abducted.'

'Abducted?' I asked, bemused. It had not occurred to me that the family would be unaware of his death, but Song's son seemed clueless. 'How old were you?'

'I was five. I've no memory of him.'

'Not unusual for a five-year-old.' I nodded and tried to accept that hiding such a terrible truth from a five-year-old was the kindest thing to do. But he was now forty-three. There comes an age when the truth ceases to be upsetting and must be known.

'You are the baby of the family? Did they spoil you a bit?' That was the extent to which I could express my discontent. He couldn't have read my thoughts but still looked at me askance.

'Being spoiled probably only applies to wealthy families—don't you think?'

'Your mom must have had a very difficult time.'

'Unspeakably. She was left all alone with five children. My eldest brother was only in high school.'

'What a woman, to have managed on her own.'

'My brother deserves some credit too. He quit school to help put food on the table. My mother and brother did all the work, but I'm the one that got an education. It feels awful, benefitting from all his toils, taking care of my mother, and now with my father's book…'

That was why he had reached out to me. At his brother's behest, he had collated all of Song's literary labours—one full-length novel and about forty short stories and novellas—which he wanted to collect into a three-part set. After all these years, only now were they able to entertain the idea, due in no small part to the recent upsurge of previously banned books newly published in the authors' real names. But Song's works had little commercial potential, much as in the past, and had been stiff-armed by every publisher they had approached.

So the oldest son now wanted to publish it out of his own pocket, which I supposed meant he must be comfortably well-off. He had a petrol station in a satellite city of Seoul and ran an auto parts shop in the city centre, which made him the most self-made out of all his siblings. From me, he wanted the cherry on top—the words of Song's contemporaries and a student of his who had become a writer. He said a novelist and a poet who were friends of his father's had gladly accepted his request. For me, he suggested a foreword in the form perhaps of an open letter.

'How would I write a letter...'

I stopped myself from asking how a letter could be written to the afterworld.

'His poet friend will largely rely on personal anecdotes, which I think will give a sense of my father's human side. The novelist friend will discuss his work. So you could focus on his family—us. Celebrate how we were able to republish his work. Things like that. You could do that? A little awkward for us to say it ourselves, you see. It would be great if you could say something too about how big of an influence he was for your writing career perhaps?'

It was a fully scripted plan and there was no reason for me to reject a part in it if it was for Song. But how could I possibly pretend that Song was still in North Korea, knowing he was dead? It would be adding another layer of lies on top of Q's error, much less correcting it.

I told him I would write the letter. I thought about whether I should address it to *Song in the North or to Song in the afterworld,* though the specifics of the address were of little importance. Yet when I sat down to write, I could not leave it undetermined. To do right by his family would be to nod along to a blatant lie. But I cared more about Song than about his surviving family.

There was no need for grandeur or glamour, because a repository for his life's work would reflect how any hint of excess, both in person and on paper, made him shudder. In Korean class, his lessons on sentence-making always warned against frothy prose. He had no patience for pomposity or vanity or ornament in the writing of young students. What would he say to these self-indulgent games of old men? Even with greying hair, his eyes never lost focus.

It was possible that a gentle cover-up by Song's wife for the sake of her young children could have hardened into an established fact. I could only imagine how a death sentence in

the family for acting for the communists would have continued to
haunt a family for generations. So it could have been swept under
the rug as an act of motherly protection. But the children were not
children anymore. The youngest of the bunch was well into his
forties, they should be able to understand the era of their father
and how and why it had extinguished him. It was no longer a
matter of shame or pride. All they needed to do was look the truth
directly in the eye.

So, regardless of the family's wishes, I set my heart on
restoring the finale of Song's life in his collected works. And for
that I needed a third party to corroborate what I knew to be true.
Because as long as Song's wife refused to admit it, I would remain
the only person in the world to know the truth.

When the United Nations Forces recaptured Seoul on 28
September 1950, it was, in my experience, far more joyous than the
end of the Japanese occupation. The citizenry, no longer starved
or in fear, was hungry for vengeance. They wanted to weed out
the sympathisers, and any accusation of being a 'commie' could
get you noosed. You were lucky to get away with a beating or to
be tried before a judge, but plenty were eliminated instantly by
vigilante youth gangs or the army. Lawless cruelty was the byword
of the day.

My own uncle was arrested for being a communist
sympathiser. At the time, he was a high street wholesaler but
closed up as soon as the chaos bore down. His spacious shop
was seized by the North Korean army to use as shelter and to
store plundered munitions and horses. When they demanded three
meals a day, it would be all hands on deck to prepare the food.
The silver lining was they never worried about going hungry.

This was my uncle's only offence, to help in these
preparations, but he was ratted out by a neighbour and taken away.

My uncle managed to avoid summary judgement or execution and was detained in Seodaemun Prison awaiting trial. Because my cousin was too young, I was responsible for supplying him food and clothing but the prison was jam-packed with the accused and didn't allow visits. The whole area was chaotically crowded with prisoners' families vying for access. To deliver clothing, I would have to spend the night at a nearby inn and depart for the prison as soon as curfew hours passed, and even then there was no knowing whether I would get a turn to make the delivery. Relatives of the accused were treated like swine. All we wished for in those days was somehow to get to know someone on the inside, a prison guard perhaps.

The prisoners were transported to courts on pickup trucks and hooded so that they couldn't be recognised. Family members would follow without knowing the date of the trials, hoping the prisoners might be able to see them through the slits of their hood. That is when I spotted Mrs Song, who was there for the same reason I was. She was no longer the elegantly modest housewife I had remembered her to be. My transformation must have been even more drastic because she didn't recognise me at all. Nor did she care as she nodded through my re-introduction without really listening; she grabbed my hand and took me to a quiet place, to ask for a favour. She drew a folded letter from her waist pocket. A petition. On the bottom were printed names of some literary giants, the high school headmaster, and several teachers.

Song had not hidden from the chaos of the battles in Seoul and instead had continued going to the school or the literary alliance office. He hadn't done anything in particular during that time but after Seoul was recaptured he felt he could not face his students and spent his days at home in self-reproach. The fact his colleagues visited often to prompt him to return signalled that whatever he had done was clearly not serious but still he somehow ended up in prison. Mrs Song failed to get any of the names printed to sign which was why she was asking for my help. A pleading student could perhaps convince at least some fellow teachers, she hoped. I politely declined due to my own circumstances as my uncle's caretaker.

'One of them must be the informer,' Mrs Song said bitterly, shaking the crumpled envelope. She deeply begrudged the people who would not sign. I was afraid that my rejection would embitter her further, and towards me too, and left in a hurry. That was the last I saw of her though it may be I avoided her on purpose after that.

I had not been aware of my uncle's trial date but received a letter from him through a released inmate. Inside the yellowing envelope, his message, written in pencil, was pithy and pitiful.

*A death sentence. How indifferent the universe is. Please find me a lawyer. I do not want to die like a beast. Song was also executed.*

*I got the jacket, but the cotton lining is too thin. I'd like it to be thicker.*

We couldn't grant any of his requests. As temperatures dipped, word was going around that inmates were transferred to prisons deeper south, but we had no way to be sure. My family got no notice whether he was killed or had died from illness, but he could be found neither in nor outside prison ever since. We had to leave my uncle to fate. It might be hard to believe, but our destitution was as brutal as his. My uncle might have died like a beast, but we were living like one.

So Song's death was indisputable, but the witness to his death was no longer among us either. Then I was reminded of another witness.

Back when even the inmates were being evacuated from Seoul, our family seemed to be almost the only ones left. In that vacuum, makeshift markets cropped up where people bartered small goods, and I went, not so much out of need but as to prove to myself that there were other people remaining besides just us. There, I ran into Hyejin, a friend from high school. She couldn't have sounded more cheerful despite her wan complexion and frostbite sprouting on her hands which gave her a strange air. After high school, she chose to help with housework instead of going to university. She joined a neighbourhood youth league when the war broke, which eventually landed her in prison. When she was released her family had already fled and she was too bone-tired to set out to find them, but their house still had a stockpile of food so she decided to stay.

'I haven't seen my family yet but it feels unreal to be back out. You have no idea how many people die in there. Mr Song passed away too,' she had said, her eyes welling up.

These were things I already knew, so I simply listened. Despite men and women being detained separately, the cells were so choked that it was possible to hear wardens' roll calls. She was at first troubled to hear the name of the man who had been her teacher just half a year before, she had said, but then a terrible emptiness came over her when his name was no longer called. According to prison hearsay, he had been executed, not released. Once this memory surfaced to the front of my mind, I instantly made contact with some old friends to get a hold of Hyejin's number. She picked up, sounding excited to hear from me.

'Good heavens! How long has it been? We haven't seen each other since... graduation, it must have been?'

'Didn't we see each other just after the third battle of Seoul?'
I said, which seemed to set her teeth on edge.

'Ah, yes. I suppose that was it. Why did you call me?'

'I'm trying to confirm something about Song. Something you told me. Perhaps not over the phone? Let's meet up sometime. We can catch up,' I said chattily.

'Look,' she said. 'What are you playing at?' She sounded more collected than before, but I could hear a tremor in her voice.

'Hyejin, are you okay?'

'My husband doesn't know I was locked up. He, his entire family—they don't have a clue, but my life has been just fine. I'm not sure what you're waiting for me to say, but what makes you think I'll talk? Go write your little novels instead of digging up other people's secrets,' she said and hung up.

Stunned, I was still in a stupor when she suddenly called me back.

'I want to apologise. I was so startled. I panicked. I wasn't in my right mind. It's just that you and my family are the only ones who know about my past. I'll do anything to stop it spreading, not that you would do that. You haven't told anyone, have you? Thank god, let's keep it that way. And it might be better if we don't contact each other again. It isn't great to feel like someone has something on you, as you know. Anyway, I trust you. Again, sorry for the way I spoke to you earlier.'

I found it harder to listen to her grovelling pleas than her fits of anger but I gave in to them and swore, as she wanted. By then, my vision of restoration had already halfway receded.

A few days later, it all flooded back when I ran into Baek Min-sae at a cocktail party. The old man could be of help, I thought. Once a novelist, Baek set foot in government in the early sixties and assumed a string of top-flight bureaucratic posts after which he enjoyed a comfortable retirement. What piqued my interest was not so much the course of his high-flying career, but his name on Mrs Song's petition. His name, which she had scrawled on the very first line, was one she had scorned for being particularly hostile to her.

This is not to say my intention was to confront Baek about the matter or speak ill of him. Baek would know better than anyone that Song was detained immediately upon arrest, with no time for him to have been whisked to the North. Even if he weren't apprised of Song's death, I would have accomplished a small mission if he could be persuaded to at least testify to Song's detainment.

The party was occasioned by the anniversary of a daily newspaper and was heaving. I would often receive invitations to similar events but had never attended one. It was bewildering, and I was slightly put out that my writer friend had changed our meeting spot from the city centre to this melee.

'Don't be a square. It's a free dinner and interesting company. We can go somewhere else afterwards.'

'You know I'm not one for this kind of revelry.'

'You're just tense about feeling more alone in the crowd. Don't worry—I'll be right by your side,' she assured me, before slithering her way through the crush of people, striking up conversation after conversation, and I found myself completely alone. As people often do when they find themselves alone, I looked around aimlessly. I then spotted Baek cackling amid a group of elderly gentlemen and made a beeline for him and introduced myself. What an honour to meet you, I told him. The reverential tone came bafflingly easy. I fawned over his early works, and his silver-haired entourage joked about how unfair I was being to those who had never produced a novel in their salad days. Then they exchanged knowing looks before doddering away one by one, and I could get to the point.

'You knew Song Sa-muk, the writer.'

'Of course,' he said. 'I practically made him. Such a shame that a great talent like his was snatched.'

A familiar drift.

'Snatched?' I said, as if trying to hold onto an eel slipping from my grasp. But resignation quickly set in. 'Surely you're aware that's not the truth.'

'Some say that he defected, but how dare they! Can you believe the insolence? He would never go to the North of his own volition. Never mind whether he defected, or whether he was abducted for that matter. I just hope he's still alive. A friend of mine with American residency visits North Korea every now and then and I am always keen to enquire about Song's whereabouts, so far to no avail. This is not because of any particular ineptitude on the part of my friend but because the society there, by all accounts, is simply inconceivable. Inconceivable indeed, to us and our logic. Look at how they just carted off such a good-natured and worldly man as Song. How did you know him, by the way?' he finally asked, after babbling on for much longer than necessary.

I could not bear to look at him with all his dissembling and the elegance with which he wore his old age. Instead, I fixed my gaze on the martini glass balanced on the palm of one hand as he twirled its stem with the fingers of the other. From this meaningless fiddling, I desperately tried to read what he was really thinking. But when another younger guest approached to exchange pleasantries, Baek seized on it as an opportunity to turn away from me and forget that I existed at all.

The letter I was to write had me stumped at the first line. Still torn between addressing it to Song in the *North and Song in the afterworld,* I blew the deadline by double the amount of time I had been given. Still, I didn't hear from Song's son. Not a peep.

Since it wasn't a periodical with a set hour to go to press, I thought they could have made changes to their plans or even scrapped the project altogether. It wasn't itself something for me to be hung up on, but the unwritten first line had begun to hold me back from doing anything else.

When Song's son finally got in touch, I was the one hectoring him.

'What happened? It's long past the publication date.'

'Well, we haven't received your foreword yet...'

'Isn't it your responsibility to chase it down?'

'There's no rush,' he said. 'It's not as if we're loan sharks or something.'

From his tone, I was not sure they had any intent to publish at all, which enraged me beyond reason.

'Then why did you call? Is this not about the manuscript?'

'Well, my brother asked to see you.'

"And why is that?"

'It seems he wants to invite you to dinner, for your trouble. We've been demanding favours without proper introduction.'

'So this is about the manuscript.'

'No, not at all.'

'It's alright. Let's call it what it is.'

'I apologise. My brother can be that way. He's a businessman.'

'And a businessman would get straight down to business.'

So that is how I ended up at a chophouse in the Gangnam district with Song's eldest son, a typical smooth-talking salesman with a paunch. He slid me a business card that listed several companies.

'I'm out of the red now, but back when things were rough and I was coming up with business ideas that went nowhere, I considered becoming a writer,' he said. 'Much easier said than done. But I still have my father's blood running through my veins, and I still have a great deal of admiration for your lot. Very pleased to have you here.'

The more fluently he flattered me, the more careful I was to not fall for it. Without mincing my words, I asked, 'How much do you know about your father?'

'Let's see… I was fifteen when he passed…'

'So you're aware that he passed away.'

'Of course. How could I not know?'

'Your youngest brother didn't seem to…'

'Yes, that. He calls it a kidnapping. That's a little euphemism within the family. It's much nicer than 'execution' or 'death in custody'.'

'A euphemism?'

'Yes, a euphemism. Or perhaps more a tacit agreement, if you will. But it's not something my family came up with. A while back, works by writers who defected to the North were compiled, and it included our father, so we just decided to go with it.'

'But why be complicit in a lie about your own family? Aren't you in the best position to correct it?'

'Had it been something to celebrate, we would've wanted to stand out. But if not, it's easier to fall in with the majority. You can think of it as a coping strategy. It's bad enough we had to deal with the misfortune in the first place, so let's at least not single it out as something unusual.'

I had wanted to discuss whether to open the letter with *Dear Song in the North* or *Dear Song in the afterworld.* Instead, I found myself ravenously nibbling on the ribs.

Everybody looks for an escape plan, a trapdoor, as if the truth is nothing more than a snare. I wasn't the one to point the finger, not with my big mouth. It might have been that I kept on nibbling so that my big mouth would stay shut in front of him.

34     Song's eldest son was now busy detailing the hard-earned achievements of his siblings. One of his brothers, who had only a vocational school degree, got a job at a large company and worked his way up to being a factory manager. His two sisters had also only completed high school but one was married to a professor and the other to an entrepreneur and both now flaunted their enviably comfortable lives. The wife of his youngest brother—the one I'd met—was from a family of intellectuals and was working towards a doctorate degree herself. He wanted me to reel off this list of the five children's triumphs in my letter. And he was bribing me with something as trifling as a plate of grilled ribs and a bottle of soju.

I started to laugh indiscriminately and repeatedly raised my glass.

A toast, to what cannot be restored.

복원되지 못한 것들을 위하여

# Iyagi — Chapbook Series

**Iyagi** is a series of chapbooks
showcasing the work of some of the
most exciting writers working in Korean
today, published by Strangers Press,
part of the UEA Publishing Project.

It is our latest collaboration with an
international group of independent
creative practitioners and all made
possible by generous funding from
LTI Korea.

For That Which Cannot Be Restored
Park Wanseo

Translated from Korean by
Soobin Kim

First published by
Strangers Press, Norwich, 2023
part of the UEA Publishing Project

Distributed by
BookSource, UK

This book is published with the support
of the Literature Translation Institute of Korea

Printed by
Swallowtail Print, Norwich

Series editors
Nathan Hamilton & Anton Hur

Cover design and typesetting
studio aono-billson

Typefaces
Roboto / Roboto Mono
Nanum Gothic

Illustration and Design, Copyright © Nigel Aono-Billson, 2023

ISBN: 978-1-913861-53-7

LTI KOREA 한국문학번역원

strangers press

UEA
University of East Anglia

UEA PUBLISHING PROJECT
NORWICH